First published in 1990
Copyright © Anthony Kerins 1990
All rights reserved
Printed in Italy
for J.M. Dent & Sons Ltd
91 Clapham High Street
London SW4 7TA

British Library Cataloguing in Publication Data
Kerins, Anthony
    Lost.
    I. Title
    823'.914 [J]
    ISBN 0-460-88004-7

Illustrated in full colour in gouache.

L O S T

Anthony Kerins

J.M. Dent & Sons Ltd · London

Every summer Callie went to stay with her Gran who lived by the sea. Each day they would spend hours on the beach together. Callie loved the feel of the hot sand between her toes and the cool splash of the sea when the tide came in.

Even when it rained Gran and Callie went to the beach. They squelched their boots in the wet sand, and watched the waves crashing on the shore. Callie loved the beach.

One hot afternoon, when the sand was so dry that all her castles crumbled, Callie set off to fill her bucket with sea-water. Suddenly she heard music. It was coming from a roundabout and she could see its shiny top flashing in the sunlight.

"Gran! Gran!" she called, "there's a roundabout on the beach. Please can I have a ride on it?"

But Gran didn't answer. She had fallen asleep. "Gran?" said Callie again, but there was still no answer.

Callie slumped down by her Gran's
chair and started to dig. She couldn't
help twisting around to look at the
roundabout.
"It's really very close," she thought.

Callie glanced again at Gran who was
still fast asleep. Then, all on her own,
Callie walked to the roundabout.

It was brilliant! There were trains and tigers and all sorts of other things to sit in. She chose a yellow helicopter, and climbed into it.

The roundabout started to move. Callie laughed with delight. Round and round, faster and faster she whirled.

When the ride was over, Callie felt dizzy but she was having fun. Setting off to find Gran, she saw some children jumping off a post. Callie was puzzled because she couldn't remember passing them on the way to the roundabout. She stopped for a moment.

"Do you want a turn?" called one of the children.
"Oh, yes please," said Callie.
She jumped off the top and joined the line again –
once, twice, three times, before she remembered
Gran. She thought she'd better hurry back to her.

Callie left the children and went further along the
beach but she could not see Gran anywhere. Callie
looked this way and that, trying to remember where
Gran had been sitting. Suddenly she saw the back of
her red chair, and laughed with relief.

But the chair was empty. Gran wasn't there! Callie didn't know what to do, so she sat down by the chair to wait, but she couldn't sit still.

Where could Gran be? Callie began to feel afraid – perhaps Gran was lost? Callie decided to find her.

She walked along the beach staring at all the people. Callie
carried on and on, but Gran was nowhere to be seen.

Everyone around her seemed to be so tall and noisy. There were big girls and babies, boys and grown-ups all running and splashing and laughing with each other. But she didn't know any of them.

Callie felt so lonely.

She walked until the soft sand ended. This part of
the beach had hard stones that hurt her feet. There
weren't so many people here, but still she couldn't
see Gran.

Callie turned round. She started to cry; big sobs that made her catch her breath. She sat down.
Callie was lost.

Suddenly she heard a shout.
It sounded like Gran.
"Callie!"
Callie spun round.
"Gran! Gran!" she yelled.
Gran hugged her granddaughter hard.
"Oh Callie! Where have you been? I've been
looking for you everywhere!"
Callie laughed and cried, and cried and laughed,
"I've found you, Gran! I've found you!"
"But don't you ever go off and leave me like
that again!"